To Lydie and Eugenia, to Anna, Alexandra, and Ingo, to Apollo, Artemis, and Tsetsa. — V.R., C.R.

HIP HOP

WORDS BY CHRIS RASCHKA

DOG

PICTURES BY VLADIMIR RADUNSKY

HARPER

An Imprint of HarperCollinsPublishers

Let me **bowwow** my life story,

From its **rudeness** to its **gladness**.

It's a **doggy** allegory,

Oh my **goodness**, oh my **badness**.

You just **sit** and perk your **ears up**,

Keep your **paws** still if you're **able**.

Get the **skinny** on **this here pup**

While I **bark** this canine **fable**.

saddest. I'm the lowest and the slowest, never yes-est, always no-est, I'm the one-est,

why I'm the Hip Hop Dog

Now I **wander** as I **wonder**
At the **pugs** and Irish **setters**.

So I **ponder**, did I **blunder**?
Am I **just** a **no-go-getter**?

When I **spot** a Weimaraner,
Cocker **spaniel,** and a **Shih Tzu,**

Taller, higher, smarter, blonder,
Makes me **bite** and I could **spit, too.**

I'm the **sad**dest and the **bad**dest, and the **bad**dest and the **call**-est. **Now** do you see not the **tall**est, least of **all**-est, wish you'd **call**-est.

saddest. I'm the leanest and the meanest, not the cleanest cocoa bean-est, I'm the smallest

why I am the Hip Hop Dog?

So I **slink** amid the **gutters**,
Trash-can **bangers**, and street **chatter**,

Through the **clink** of sidewalk **clutter**,
But that **clatter** makes me **gladder**;

So much **gladder** that I **woof**—
And I **arf, pant, huff,** and **growl.**
Now I'll **shout** and raise the **roof**
With one good **maxi**-canine **howl.**

oo oo rrrr wowf wowf wowf ee ee ah ah

Maybe it's all right to be the Hip

arf boot boot boot boof. Maybe it's all

ah ah bowf bowf bowf gr gr m' m' m' m' zoof zoof zoof zoof zoof

Hop Dog.

zoof zoof ha ha 'airf 'airf 'airf ha ha zoof zoof zoof zoof

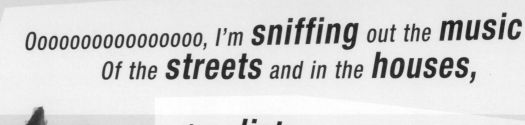

Ooooooooooooooooo, I'm **sniffing** out the **music**
Of the **streets** and in the **houses**,

And I **listen** to the **squeaking**
Of the **cats** and of the **mouses**.

I like **Louis**, I dig **bop**,
But then I **stop** because I **smelled** a

Something **funky** at the **opera**;
Now I **bark** it like **Brünhilda**.

I'm the **zoom**-est and the **boom**-est, spread no **gloom**-est,

Hip Hop

like it as the

I like it as

I jazzle dazzle

say no **doom**-est. I'm the **top**-est, never **stop**-est, Boston **pop**-est, be be **bop**-est.

Dog.

Now the **pit bulls** and the **schnoodles**
Know I'm **not** some lowly **mutt.**

All the **Afghans** and the **poodles**
Like to **stop** and watch me **strut,**

As I **mark** my **territory,**
Turning **heads** on all the **breeders;**

When I **make** it **auditory,**
If there's a **pack,** then I'm the **leader.**

oo oo rrrr wowf wowf wowf ee ee ah ah ah ah ah ah

boof boof

arf boof

arf arf arf

ah ah bowf bowf bowf bowf gr gr gr w' w' w' w' zoof zoof zoof zoof ha ha zoof zoof ha

boof.

I'm the **COOL**est, I'm the **quick**est and the **slick**est, **rule**-est. I'm the **bright**est, no need t' **fight**-est, pure de**light**-est, y'know I'm the **Hippy** Hippy Hippy Hippy Hippy Hippy Hip Hop Dog Hip Hop Dog, **right**-est. I'm the **bright**-est, no need t' fight-est, pure de**light**-est, y'know I'm the finger-**lick**-est, **lick**-est. I'm the **right**-est, finger-**tic**-est, **tocky**-tic-est, **rule**-est doggies doggies-**lick** not a **fool**-est, doggies

go to **school**-est.

Library of Congress Cataloging-in-Publication Data

Raschka, Christopher.

  Hip hop dog / written by Chris Raschka ; illustrated by Vladimir Radunsky. — 1st ed.

   p. cm.

  Summary: A neglected dog finds his purpose through rapping and rhyming.

  ISBN 978-0-06-123963-2 (trade bdg.)

  ISBN 978-0-06-123964-9 (lib. bdg.)

  [1. Stories in rhyme. 2. Dogs—Fiction. 3. Hip-hop—Fiction.

4. Rap (Music)—Fiction.] I. Radunsky, Vladimir, ill. II. Title.

PZ8.3.R1768Hi 2009   2008031449

[E]—dc22   CIP

                        AC

Book design by Vladimir Radunsky

Prepress by Katharina Gasterstadt

10 11 12 13 14   LEO   10 9 8 7 6 5 4 3 2 1

❖

First Edition